Thurgood Marshall
Supreme Court Justice

Emilio Chavez

Infomax Readers

Rosen Classroom™

New York

Published in 2014 by The Rosen Publishing Group, Inc.
29 East 21st Street, New York, NY 10010

Book Design: Mickey Harmon

Photo Credits: Bachrach/Contributor/Archive Photos/Getty Images; cover, pp. 3, 4, 6, 8, 10, 12, 14, 16, 18, 20, 22–24 (background) Attitude/Shutterstock.com; pp. 3, 4, 6, 8, 10, 12, 14–16, 18, 20, 22–24 (paper texture) akkaradech/Shutterstock.com; p. 5 Charles Tasnadi/APImages.com; p. 7 Hank Walker/Contributor/Time & Life Pictures/Getty Images; p. 9 New York Times Co./Contributor/Archive Photos/Getty Images; p. 11 Onur ERSIN/Shutterstock.com; p. 13 Library of Congress/Wikipedia.org; p. 17 Ed Clark/Contributor/Time & Life Pictures/Getty Images; p. 19 Keystone/Stringer/Hulton Archive/Getty Images; p. 21 Stock Montage/Contributor/Archive Photos/Getty Images; p. 22 Cynthia Johnson/Contributor/TIME & LIFE Images/Getty Images.

ISBN: 978-1-4777-2599-3
6-pack ISBN: 978-1-4777-2600-6

Manufactured in the United States of America

CPSIA Compliance Information: Batch #CS13RC: For further information contact Rosen Publishing, New York, New York at 1-800-237-9932.

Contents

Who Was Thurgood Marshall?

Maya's mom loves reading biographies. A biography is the story of somebody's life. She just finished reading about Thurgood Marshall. Maya has never heard of him. She asks her mom, "Who was Thurgood Marshall?"

"Thurgood Marshall was America's first African American Supreme Court justice," says Maya's mom. "His work as a **lawyer** helped him get there." Maya can't wait to hear more about his life!

Thurgood Marshall did many great things in his life.

The Marshall Family

Thurgood Marshall was born on July 2, 1908. He grew up in Baltimore, Maryland, with his mom, dad, and older brother, William. His dad worked for a railroad, and his mom was a kindergarten teacher.

Thurgood's dad liked watching lawyers argue cases at the local courthouse. He told Thurgood and William about the cases he saw. They would talk about them for hours. Maya's mom asks her, "How do you think this affected Thurgood's life?"

Thurgood learned to respect our country's laws because of the example his dad set.

A Tough Time

Thurgood grew up at a time when African Americans were **discriminated** against because of their skin color. Blacks were kept separate from whites. There were laws that made it this way.

"Thurgood was black, so he knew how unfair discrimination was," says Maya's mom. "This made him want to become a lawyer. Being a lawyer would help him change laws that treated people unfairly."

Because blacks were discriminated against, they couldn't go to white businesses. They had to ride in the back of buses, and their schools had less money.

PARAMOUNT THEATRE
COLORED ENTRANCE
Enjoy Good Shows in Comfort

School Days

Thurgood was a good student, but sometimes he caused trouble! In high school, a teacher made him learn the entire **Constitution** because he acted out in class. Maya's mom says, "Thurgood didn't think this was bad. In fact, knowing the Constitution helped him later in life."

Thurgood finished high school in 1925 and went on to **college**. He studied at Lincoln University in Pennsylvania. His grades were good enough for our country's best law schools. "He must've been very smart," Maya says.

It wasn't easy for African Americans to get into law school, but Thurgood knew he could do it.

We the People
insure domestic Tranquility, provide for the common
and our Posterity, do ordain and establish this Constitution
Article 1

After college, Thurgood applied to the University of Maryland Law School. His grades were good, but they wouldn't let him in because he was black. Maya's mom explains, "Although it was unfair, it was the law."

Thurgood went to Howard University Law School instead. He worked with the school's dean, or leader, Charles Houston. Thurgood learned a lot from Charles. They worked together later in life. Thurgood finished law school in 1933 and opened his own law office.

Thurgood became a lawyer so he could work on discrimination cases. His work made him famous.

STAMP OUT
GEORGE W. LEE
LAMAR SMITH
EMMETT TILL
CLINTON MELTON
JOIN
NAACP
NATIONAL ASSOCIATION FOR THE ADVANCEMENT OF COLORED PEOPLE

Thurgood, the Lawyer

Thurgood became a lawyer for a group called the National Association for the Advancement of Colored People (NAACP). The NAACP worked with people who faced discrimination. For his first case, Thurgood helped a man named Donald Murray.

Donald applied to the University of Maryland Law School, but he was kept out because he was black. "That's just like what happened to Thurgood," Maya says. Thurgood showed this was unfair and won the case in 1935. It was the first of many he would win.

Thurgood's Cases

1935

Murray v. Pearson
Showed it was wrong to keep black students like Donald from attending the University of Maryland Law School.

1940

Chambers v. Florida
Proved that four black men were wrongly blamed for a crime.

1954

Brown v. Board of Education
Showed that going to separate schools meant black students got a worse education than white students.

Thurgood worked on many cases. Here are some of the most important.

In 1954, Thurgood won a very important case. It was called *Brown v. Board of Education*. Maya's mom says, "Thurgood had to show it was wrong for black students and white students to go to separate schools." It was wrong because black schools were usually worse than white schools.

"Did he win the case?" asks Maya.

"He did," says her mom. The decision made it illegal for blacks to be treated differently in schools than whites. It was an important moment in the fight for **civil rights**.

Thurgood became a lawyer so he could fight for equality. Winning this case showed it was possible.

Noticed by Presidents

Many people noticed how special Thurgood was, including our presidents! President John F. Kennedy made him a judge for the United States government in 1961. Then, he became a lawyer for our government in 1965.

Maya's mom says, "These jobs are hard for anybody to get. It was especially hard for African Americans." Thurgood was one of the first African Americans to earn such high positions in the government. He made it possible for other people to do the same.

"President Lyndon B. Johnson gave Thurgood a very important job. Can you guess what it was?" asks Maya's mom.

Lyndon B. Johnson

Two years later, Thurgood made history. President Lyndon B. Johnson chose him as a Supreme Court justice. Thurgood was the first African American on the U.S. Supreme Court. He began this position on October 2, 1967.

Maya learned about the Supreme Court in school. It makes decisions on very important court cases. Lawyers and judges have to be smart and fair in order to become part of the Supreme Court. Maya tells her mom, "I think Thurgood was both of these things."

Thurgood made it possible for other African Americans to do great things.

Remembering a Hero

Thurgood worked as a Supreme Court justice until 1991. He died two years later, on January 24, 1993. He was 84 years old. Today, there are many schools and buildings named after him. Maya's mom says, "This is a great way to honor his memory."

Thurgood did many great things with his life. He used his position as a lawyer to win equal rights for all Americans. His lifelong love and respect for our country's laws helped him make life better for all of us.

Glossary

civil rights (SIH-vuhl RYTS) The rights of citizens to have freedom and equality.

college (KAH-lihj) The school after high school.

Constitution (kahn-stuh-TOO-shun) The writing that lists the basic laws of the United States.

discriminate (dihs-KRIH-muh-nayt) To treat somebody unfairly because they are different.

lawyer (LOY-uhr) A person who practices law.

Index